MIMI
MEMAW
YAYA
GAGA
NANA
GRANNY
BIG MAMA
AND ME

Published by Iselyn Hamilton-Austin
Library of Congress Control Number 2021901177

Printed in the United States of America
ISBN-13: 978-1-7365386-0-9

Illustrations and book cover design done by Shada L. Thomas
Art Queen Graphix, LLC

This book was given to:

From:

This book is dedicated to
Jael and Jeremiah,
my two heartbeats, who affectionately
call me MIMI and are my
inspiration for writing this book.

Being a MIMI is one of the best things
that has ever happened to me,
other than being a parent.

Love you forever, MIMI.

Whatever you are affectionately called by your grandchildren, pick from our list to read and join the fun.

Mommy and daddy asked GOD for me

And I have a

MIMI
MEMAW
YAYA
GAGA
NANA
GRANNY
BIG MAMA

That we go to see.

She gives me a bath to help keep me clean.

Scrub, scrub, scrub,

With kisses and hugs.

Love, love, love.

My

MIMI
MEMAW
YAYA
GAGA
NANA
GRANNY
BIG MAMA

AND ME.

She brushes my teeth

To help keep them clean.

There will be no cavities for

MIMI
MEMAW
YAYA
GAGA
NANA
GRANNY
BIG MAMA

AND ME.

Feeding me breakfast,

I love eggs with some cheese,

To start off the day.

Just my

MIMI
MEMAW
YAYA
GAGA
NANA
GRANNY
BIG MAMA

AND ME.

She bakes me cookies

And sneaks me some treats,

But gives me my veggies,

My beans, and my peas.

Just keeping me healthy

My

MIMI
MEMAW
YAYA
GAGA
NANA
GRANNY
BIG MAMA

AND ME.

Off to the park, to play on the swings,

Whee, Whee, Whee.

Just my

MIMI
MEMAW
YAYA
GAGA
NANA
GRANNY
BIG MAMA

AND ME.

Riding my bike

And I scraped my knee,

Fixing my boo-boo.

It's

MIMI
MEMAW
YAYA
GAGA
NANA
GRANNY
BIG MAMA

AND ME.

We stopped for some lunch

And ate under a tree.

Oh, what fun!!

Just my

MIMI
MEMAW
YAYA
GAGA
NANA
GRANNY
BIG MAMA

AND ME.

ABCDEFG

Learning my letters

My

MIMI
MEMAW
YAYA
GAGA
NANA
GRANNY
BIG MAMA

AND ME.

HIJKLMNOP

Doing so good! Oh, can you see!!

QRS TUV

Im getting better Oooh, Whee!

WXY and Z

I did it, I did it!!!

Just my

MIMI
MEMAW
YAYA
GAGA
NANA
GRANNY
BIG MAMA

AND ME.

Learning my numbers,

My ones, twos, and threes.

I can count to 100.

Just my

MIMI
MEMAW
YAYA
GAGA
NANA
GRANNY
BIG MAMA

AND ME.

Bedtime stories

And time for some ZZZZZs,

Saying my prayers.

Just my

MIMI
MEMAW
YAYA
GAGA
NANA
GRANNY
BIG MAMA

AND ME.

Tomorrow's a new day,

For more fun, you'll see.

Can't wait for what's in store!!

For my

MIMI
MEMAW
YAYA
GAGA
NANA
GRANNY
BIG MAMA

AND ME!

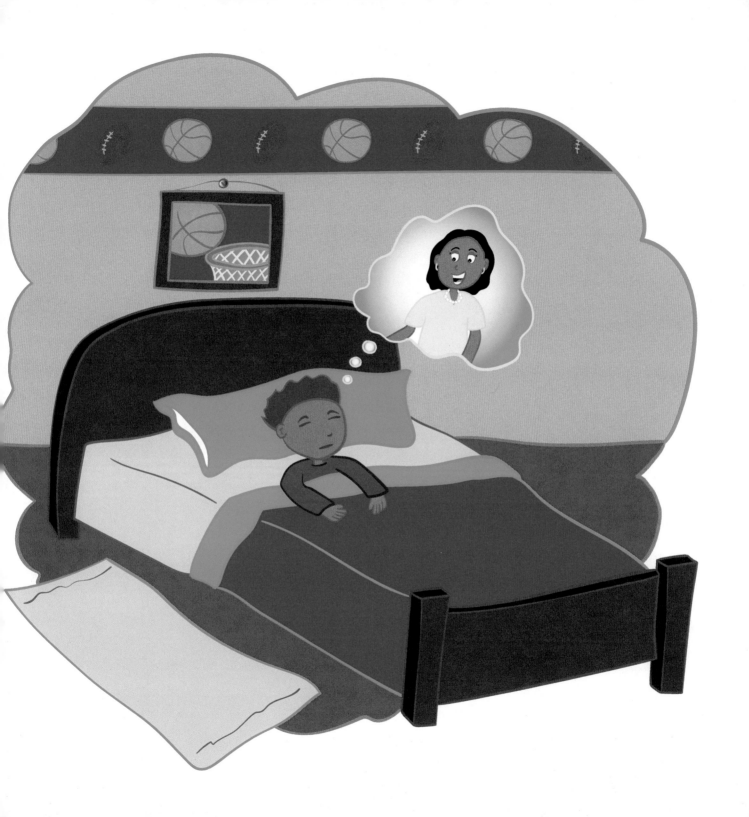

Made in United States
Orlando, FL
02 July 2022

19372533R00020